Adapted from

Grimm's Fairy Tales

HARRY N. ABRAMS, INC., PUBLISHERS, NEW YORK

ISBN 0–8109–1515–4

Times Mirror Books

Printed and bound in Japan

CHAPTER I

A LONG, long time ago, longer than anyone can possibly remember, a Queen sat by her window sewing. As her needle flashed in and out of her work, her thoughts wandered. Watching the myriads of snowflakes dancing down from the sky, she murmured:

"If I only had a little daughter I would be so happy!"

Lost in her reverie and unmindful of her work, she pricked her finger with the needle. Three drops of blood fell on the linen in her lap which was as white as the fresh-fallen snow. The bright color pleased the Queen and she exclaimed:

"How lovely my little girl would be with lips as red as blood, skin as white as snow, and hair as black as the ebony of my embroidery frame!"

In the spring, as flowers nodded in the soft breezes and birds sang in the trees, a little daughter was born to the Queen and she was all her mother had desired. But the Queen's happiness was brief. Holding her lovely baby in her arms, she whispered faintly before she died:

"Little Snow White!"

When a year had passed the lonely King took another wife. She was very beautiful, but unhappily her beauty was only a mask for a cruel, selfish heart. In no time at all she began brewing mysterious poisons to destroy the King, and when he was dead she seized the throne for herself.

The vain Queen was jealous of all the lovely ladies of her kingdom. They trembled with fear because they knew that every day the Queen looked into her magic mirror, which she prized above everything else, and asked:

"Little mirror on the wall, who is fairest of us all?"

And if the mirror replied that she was the fairest in the land, her temper was sweet and gracious all the day long. But if one of the ladies of her realm was named, the Queen fell into a terrible fury, and summoned her faithful huntsman to destroy her rival.

Thus years passed.

Meanwhile the little Princess grew more and more beautiful. Her radiant smile and sweet nature had won the hearts of everyone except the Queen, who had been too occupied with herself even to notice the child. But now Snow White's beauty alarmed her. She could never allow this child to become more beautiful than herself!

So she banished her to the servants' quarters of the castle, and made her dress in rags and slave from early morning till late at night. And while she toiled, Snow White lived in a world all her own with the people of her imagination; dreaming daydreams about a handsome young prince who fell in love with her and carried her off to his castle, far away from the dismal scullery and far, far away from the wicked Queen.

One morning as she was scrubbing in a small courtyard, Snow White sighed and sang a little song. Friendly pigeons perched close by to listen. She crossed the yard, emptied her bucket and lowered it down an old moss-covered well for fresh water. Masses of pink roses climbed over the arch above the well and framed her lovely head as she looked down, down and saw her reflection far below. Her voice echoed along the damp dark stones and seemed to come from some distant place. The pigeons chirped and nodded as she sang:

"Want to know a secret,
Promise not to tell?
We're standing by a wishing well!
Make a wish into the well,
That's all you have to do!
And if you hear it echoing,
Your wish will soon come true."

It so happened that while the little ragged princess sang under the roses, a neighboring prince neared the castle. Passing travelers in his kingdom had brought tales of the gentle Princess who was so lovely to look upon. So the Prince set out, mounted upon his white horse. Ascending the long hill by the outer wall of the castle he vowed to himself that were she half so sweet and only half so beautiful as he had heard, he would win her for his bride.

On the other side of the wall Snow White and her pigeons were leaning far over the well singing a wishing song:

"I'm wishing—
I'm wishing—(the echo answered)
For the one I love to find me—
To find me—
Today—
Today—
I'm hoping—
I'm hoping—
And I'm dreaming of
The nice things—
He'll say—
He'll say."

And suddenly another face — that of a handsome smiling Prince — was reflected beside hers in the water at the bottom of the well. Snow White stopped singing and stared in astonishment, and then turning quickly around she stood face to face with her Prince-come-true! He was real! She wasn't dreaming! He was even going to kiss her hand!

"Oh," she exclaimed. "Oh! Oh!" and ran away to the castle, up the stairs to a balcony and then peeped down. Below, the Prince looked up to her and sang:

"I've been searching everywhere
To find myself a lady fair.
Tra-la-la-la-la-la!

I'll not look any farther,
I'll win your heart and hand,
Because for me, you are
The Fairest in the Land!"

Snow White forgot she had ever been lonely. She was so happy she kissed a round white pigeon and sent it down to him. Then she disappeared through the door as fast as she could to hide her blushes.

And all the while the Queen had secretly watched the romance from her window.

She turned pale with envy, and gathering her long train over her arm she ran down the seven corridors, through the seven doors, and past the two black panthers who guarded the secret niche where her magic mirror hung.

CHAPTER II

"Mirror, mirror on the wall, who is the fairest of us all?"

A green haze slowly enveloped the glass before the mirror answered:

"Her lips blood red, her hair like night, her skin like snow, her name — SNOW WHITE!"

The angry Queen hurried from the room, calling for her huntsman.

This strong bearded man had learned to dread her summons. But he had no choice, for he well knew the penalty if he refused to obey the cruel Queen. He crossed the long halls with heavy feet and bowed low to receive her command.

"Take the Princess into the forest, and return with her heart in this jeweled box!"

A hush fell over the whole castle as the wicked order was whispered about, and in the heart of everyone was hatred for the Queen.

CHAPTER III

The dew was still on the grass the next day when Snow White rode through the palace gates with the huntsman. Birds trilled early morning songs to the sun, and in her heart Snow White sang over and over again:

"He loves me, he loves me — ah, he loves me!"

The huntsman, watching the young girl at his side with the sweet smile on her lips, wondered how anyone could wish her harm and thought to himself:

"If I kill her my soul will burn forevermore and my shame will be so great that I shall hate myself and hang my head before all men. Yet, if I fail the Queen, she will feed me to her panthers, or shrink me magically to the size of a walnut. Aye, and what will become of my poor children? And my wife? Yes, and Snow White? For the Queen will yet contrive some cruel death for her. Indeed it would be a mercy if I killed her myself!"

But as they drew closer and closer to the forest the huntsman shrank before the thought.

They entered the cool dark woods and Snow White dismounted to pick some violets. Searching among the mosses for the flowers, her fingers touched the fluffy feathers of a frightened baby bird. Still on her knees she picked it up to comfort it. Behind her the huntsman soundlessly crossed the mossy ground and slowly lifted his knife. His shadow fell over a huge rock beside the Princess. She sprang up with a cry! The knife fell out of the huntsman's hand, and as he looked into her frightened eyes, tears streamed down his rough cheeks. His voice trembled as he spoke:

"I cannot kill you even though it is the Queen's command! She's mad — she's jealous of you! Quick, child, run, run away and hide — run into the forest and never come back!"

And snatching the reins of her horse in his hand, the huntsman mounted his own horse and rode away. But he could not return the little jeweled box *empty* to the Queen. He was troubled and did not know what to do when suddenly an animal darted across the road. Taking aim he killed it and placed its heart in the box.

Then he rode back slowly to the palace.

Alone and frightened, blinded by tears, Snow White ran on and on deep into the forest. Not a ray of sunlight penetrated through the tall trees. In the gloom she tripped over an old tree root and screamed. It seemed like a monster clutching at her ankle. Her terror magnified the

shining eyes of animals and turned them into demons glaring at her. Everything came alive and seemed to be chasing her. She ran faster and faster until, breathless, she fell headlong into a swamp. With a cry of terror she scrambled from the bog only to tumble down a slope a few steps farther on. Over and over she rolled into a small clearing where she lay sobbing and shivering.

Inquisitive birds and rabbits and squirrels, and even a mother deer with her fawn, peeked out at her. But she did not see them. Her head was buried in her arms and her eyes were tight shut. A furry little rabbit, braver than the rest, nuzzled his cold nose into her neck.

"Ooooooh!" she screamed, and jumped up. Frightened, all the animals scurried off and hid. Then, as if by magic, little heads started to appear from behind leaves, out of thickets, and up from holes in the ground. In the warm sunlight Snow White saw them and laughed.

"I didn't mean to frighten you," she said.

A chipmunk parted the bunny's long ears and peeped through at her, and a baby bird hopped to the end of a branch to look down.

"And all because I was afraid. I'm so ashamed of the fuss I've made."

Looking up to the little bird, Snow White asked:

"What do you do when things go wrong?"

He raised his tiny beak and answered with a little trill.

"Oh! You sing a song!"

And Snow White smiled and sang too.

Creeping out from their hiding places, timidly at first and then boldly, came all the little animals. They clustered round her, snuggled in her lap and nestled in her arms. The birds sang with her and the air was filled with sunshine and happiness.

"I really feel quite happy now," she said. "I'm sure I'll get along somehow! And everything is going to be all right, but I do need a place to sleep tonight."

Lifting the long soft ears of the mother rabbit, she whispered:

"Maybe you know where I can stay?"

But the rabbit only twitched her pink nose and opened wide her soft round eyes.

"In the woods somewhere?" said Snow White looking around.

Her new little friends were sympathetic and grave. They hardly knew how to help her, though they wanted to.

"A woodchopper's hut would do," she suggested.

They brightened up with an idea. The birds flew off leading the way, nodding and chirping joyously. The rabbits, the chipmunks, the squirrels, and all the other little animals trooped behind Snow White who walked along with her arm around the mother deer's neck. Last of all, and far behind, plodded an old mud turtle.

Finally the procession stopped before some tall thick bushes. Grouping on either side the animals pulled apart the leaves and branches and Snow White peered through. There, in the middle of a large clearing, nestled a tiny cottage.

"Oh! It's just like a doll's house!" she exclaimed, clapping her hands with delight.

Skipping across a little bridge to the house she rubbed a spot clean on the windowpane and peeked in.

"It's dark inside!" she whispered. "Maybe there's no one home."

Straightening her rumpled dress and smoothing her hair, she knocked at the door. She knocked again, harder this time. And then she knocked very hard. But still no one came; so she turned the knob and peered in. Everything was still and quiet.

"Would it be all right if I went in and looked around?" she asked her friends.

The birds and animals all nodded "yes" and then followed close on her heels through the door.

"What a darling little chair! Why, there are *seven* little chairs! Must be seven little children!" she announced to the wide-eyed animals.

"And from the looks of this table — seven *untidy* little children! Look! A pickaxe! And a shoe! I've never seen such a mess!"

Dirty little shirts and wrinkled little trousers hung from the backs of chairs. The sink was piled high with cups and saucers and plates which looked as though they had never been washed. And everything was blanketed under a thick layer of dust.

With a deep sigh, Snow White turned to the birds and animals:

"Maybe they have no mother!" she said, "and need someone to take care of them. Let's clean the house and surprise them!"

She found a towel and tucked it around her waist for an apron. Then she started to sweep the floor while all the little animals hunted about for things to do. The squirrels busily whisked dust under the rug with their tails—until Snow White shook her finger and told them that was not the thing to do. So they swept it into a hole in the baseboard around the wall. The dust came flying back and out popped a chattering angry mouse.

High on the rafters another little squirrel busily unraveled the cobwebs and wound them into a neat ball.

And the bluebirds flew back and forth through the window to the garden, each bringing a flower in his beak. One by one they dropped them into a vase on the table until it was filled.

Snow White washed all the little shirts and trousers, using the turtle's back for a washboard, and she hung them on the mother deer's antlers to dry.

When everything was in apple-pie order, and a kettle of delicious soup was bubbling and simmering over the coals, she said to the animals:

"Let's see what's upstairs."

They all crowded up the steps. Holding the candle high, Snow White stood in the bedroom door and looked around.

"Oh! What cunning little beds," she said. "Why, they have their

names carved on them — Doc, Happy, Sneezy, Dopey . . . such funny names for children! Grumpy, Bashful and Sleepy—shhhh! I'm a little sleepy myself."

Yawning, she sank down across the beds and murmured something about children, pickaxes, shoes, and dirty dishes as she fell asleep.

The birds flew down and taking the hem of the sheet between their beaks, pulled it over her. A song rang through the forest. They cocked an ear to listen. It came nearer and nearer. The animals scampered pell-mell out of the house and the birds flew out of the window. One little bluebird darted back again and with a flick of his tail put out the candle.

Snow White didn't stir. She was sound asleep.

CHAPTER IV

"Hi-ho, hi-ho,
It's home from work we go,
Da-da-da, da-da-da-da-da,
Do-do, do-do-do-do-do-do."

Watching from behind bushes and trees and logs, the animals saw not seven little children coming out of the forest but . . . SEVEN LITTLE MEN! Each one carried a pick over his shoulder and each one could have walked under your dining room table without upsetting his cap! They all had bushy whiskers and eyebrows, and not a hair on their heads. They were the seven dwarfs. Mornings they marched off to their mines where they dug for gold and precious stones, deep down under a big mountain, and in the evening they marched back again to their little house hidden in the heart of the woods. If they had been asked what they intended to do with their piles of heaped-up treasure these funny little men would have scratched their heads and answered:

"We dunno. We never thought of that!"

Travelers never passed their cottage, and in all their hundreds of years they had never seen a woman! They believed the forest was full of dragons and demons and spooks. So you can just imagine how they felt when they saw smoke curling out of their chimney and the door standing open!

"Look! Someone's in our house . . . light's lit!"

"Maybe a ghost! . . . or a goblin! . . . or a demon!"

"Er . . . a dragon!"

"I knew it! There's trouble brewing. Felt it coming all day!" boomed Grumpy. "I've been warning you for nigh two hundred years that something awful was 'bout to happen!"

Stealing up to the door of the cottage they popped their heads in and popped them out again just as quickly.

"Nobody there!" whispered Happy.

"You can't see ghosts!" muttered Grumpy.

"Swallow me! Er . . . I mean follow me!" ordered Doc the leader, who was always getting his tongue twisted.

As they stood huddled together in the dim light, Sleepy observed: "Things look different. Sort of unhealthy!"

"Ghastly," agreed Doc. "This chair — it's been dusted!"

"Cobwebs are missing!" announced Bashful.

"There's dirty work afoot!" growled Grumpy making a fierce face. "The whole place is *clean*!"

"Sink's empty! Hey! Someone's stole our dishes!" hissed Sleepy.

"No, they're hidden in the cupboard," said Happy running his finger around a cup. "Huh! My cup's been washed — sugar's gone!"

"Psst!" said Sneezy pointing to a vase of flowers. "Look! It's full of ah-ah-ah—"

They all made a grab for Sneezy's nose but the mighty sneeze shattered the silence and blew the little men in all directions. They trembled with fear expecting the monster to leap out and destroy them.

"How do you think we can stalk this thing with you blowin' like a cyclone?" scolded Grumpy.

At that moment a weird sound came from upstairs. It was Snow White yawning and turning over in her sleep.

"It's up there!" said Doc trembling, "in the redboom . . . I mean bedroom! Sneak pup . . . peek snup . . . er . . . yes, I mean never, that is, one of us has gotta sneak up and chase it down! I'll stay here and butcher it. Who'll volunteer?"

Reaching out he grabbed Dopey's right hand and waved it in the air. Then, handing him the candle, he pushed him up the steps.

"Go on," they all whispered encouragingly, "it can't hurt you. We'll be right here!"

The candle shook violently in Dopey's hand, so violently it almost went out. As he crept into the dark bedroom, Snow White stretched her arms under the white sheet and Dopey thought it was a ghost rising from the bed. His candle flew into the air as he dashed out of the room and dove down the stairs. He landed on top of the group of wait-

ing dwarfs below, and before he could get his breath they pelted him with questions:

"Did you see it?"

"Was it a dragon?"

"Did it breathe fire?"

Dopey nodded "yes" to everything. Then he stretched out his arms as far as they would go to show how big it was and folded his hands

under his cheek and closed his eyes to show it was asleep. When they realized it was asleep the dwarfs took courage and shouldering their picks they marched right up into the bedroom. Standing on tiptoes in a circle around the beds the dwarfs stared at Snow White.

"Wha . . . what is it?" stammered Happy.

"It's mighty purty," sighed Sneezy.

"It's beautiful . . . like an angel!" said Bashful.

"But what is it?" insisted Happy.

"Why bless my soul I think, yes, that's what it is — a girl!" said Doc.

"Girl, huh!" snapped Grumpy scowling. "It's a female and all females is pizen. What's more, they're full of wicked wiles!"

"What's wicked wiles?" asked Bashful.

"I dunno, but they're mighty dangerous!" said Grumpy wagging his head. "Mark my words! We're in for a peck of trouble!"

Snow White stirred and sat up, rubbing the sleep from her eyes. And all the little dwarfs ducked down behind the beds. Then slowly seven pairs of eyes and seven red noses appeared.

"Why . . . why, you're not children!" exclaimed Snow White. "You're little men! How do you do?"

The dwarfs just stared.

"I said . . . how-do-you-do?"

"How do you do what?" snapped Grumpy.

"Oh, so you can talk!" said Snow White smiling. "I'm so glad because now you can tell me who you are." Remembering the names on the beds, she added, "But wait! Let me guess . . . you must be Doc!"

"Why-er-yes . . . YES! So I am, my dear-er-my dear!" fluttered Doc.

"And you are Bashful, aren't you?"

"Oooooooh!" giggled Bashful, squirming.

Sleepy's yawn gave him away, and Happy laughed.

"You are Happy!"

"That's me; ma'am," said Happy. "And this one's Dopey. He don't talk none." Dopey grinned from ear to ear.

"You mean he *can't* talk?" asked Snow White.

"He dunno, he never tried," broke in Sneezy. "All he can do is ah-ah-ah-ah KER CHOO!"

You're Sneezy!" laughed Snow White, and quickly changing to a mock frown, she said, "and you're Grumpy!"

"Yeh!" said Grumpy turning his back. "We know who we are. Ask her who she is and what she's doing in our house!"

"Oh! I forgot to tell you. I'm Snow White."

"*THE PRINCESS!*" they all said together.

She nodded and started to tell them of her adventures, but when she mentioned the Queen they gasped and their eyes almost popped out of their heads.

"I'm warning you!" said Grumpy. "If the wicked Queen finds out we've given shelter to this female, we'll wake up some morning and find ourselves dead!"

"Nonsense," laughed Snow White. "She doesn't even know where I am!"

"Doesn't know!" snorted Grumpy. "She knows everything! She can even make herself invisible! For all we know she may be in this very room right now!"

The men gulped and nodded, while Dopey started to peer under the beds and into old shoes, looking for her. He even looked in his pocket and under Doc's beard.

Snow White pretended to feel hurt and disappointed and walked toward the door.

"All right," she said, "I'll go. If you don't care whether the wild beasts eat me, or the demons and goblins get me, I don't want to stay. Besides why should I stay to clean house for seven little 'fraidy cats, and cook for them and . . ."

"Did you say COOK!" asked Happy.

"I can cook everything," replied Snow White with a mischievous twinkle in her eyes. "Apple dumplings, huckleberry pancakes, gooseberry pies . . ."

"GOOSEBERRY PIES!" shouted all the dwarfs. "Hurry! She stays! She stays!"

Grumpy's angry voice rose above the others as he tore his way to the middle of the group.

"Would you risk your necks for a piece of pie?" he shouted.

"*YOU BET!*" they all yelled. "It'll taste mighty good. Raisins in the crust? Melt in your mouth! You can eat 'till you bust!"

Licking his lips hungrily, Grumpy mumbled:

"Well, she can stay till we get our pie. Then out she goes!"

Just as the dwarfs were cheering loudly, Snow White smelled the soup boiling over downstairs. She screamed and flew out of the room.

They all looked after her, bewildered.

"Didn't I tell you?" sniffed Grumpy. "She's crazy. Wimmin! Pah!"

CHAPTER V

The dwarfs were curious to see what would happen next, so they crawled to the landing and stuck their heads through the spindles of the railing. Delicious soup smells floated up and tickled their noses.

"Ahhhhh . . . *SOOOUP!*" they shouted and bolted downstairs to the table — all except Dopey who was still wiggling his head out of the railing.

"Supper is not quite ready yet," said Snow White. "You'll just have time to wash."

"Wash?" stammered the little men looking from one to the other. It had been so long since any of them had really washed that they had almost forgotten what the word meant.

"Or perhaps you *have* washed?" suggested Snow White.

"Why yes, yes, perhaps we have . . . perhaps," stammered Doc.

"But when?" demanded Snow White.

"Er, ah, oh . . . recently!" said Doc.

"Humph!" sniffed Snow White. "Let me see your hands. Hold them out!"

What hands! Even the dwarfs were embarrassed and hung their heads.

"Worse than I suspected!" declared Snow White trying to be stern. "March right out and wash those hands! And behind the ears! And under the beards!"

Sheepishly the men filed out. But Grumpy was angry. He folded his arms defiantly and marched right into the door, bumping his nose.

"*Poor* Grumpy!" said Snow White.

Mad as a hornet he stalked outside and scrambled up on a barrel.

"Wimmin!" he snorted. "WIMMIN!"

Doc and the others were determined to please the Princess if it killed them — and they felt pretty sure it would! Like as not to catch rheumatism or pneumonia, that's what they were, if they weren't careful!

"Will your whiskers shrink?" spluttered Sleepy.

"Do you get in the tub?" ventured Bashful.

"Now don't get excited," said Doc. "Here you go — Bludle-bludle-bludle-blub!"

Grumpy yelled from his balcony seat:

"You bunch of old nanny goats make me sick! First thing you know the female will be tying your beards up in pink ribbons and smelling you all to high heaven with that stuff called perfume. A fine bunch of water-lilies you turned out to be! Heh! heh! I'd like to see anybody make me wash! Pah!"

"Oh!" said Doc. "All right, men, grab the old wart hog!"

They tossed Grumpy, kicking and yelling, into the tub and three men held him down while the other three went to work.

"Soap," ordered Doc, "get the soap!"

Dopey grabbed the soap but it squirted out of his hands into the air and dropped right down into his wide-open mouth! He started to hiccough and each time he said "Hic" a great big beautiful bubble floated out. Poor Dopey! He was so frightened he clapped both hands over his mouth and then the bubbles came out of his ears!

"SUPPER!" called Snow White from the doorway.

Like a hot potato Grumpy was dropped back in the tub and they all made a dive for the door.

CHAPTER VI

Meanwhile the impatient Queen walked up and down, and back and forth across the marble floors of the castle. It was very late and the huntsman had not returned. As the minutes passed she plotted a thousand tortures for him if he had failed to obey her command.

A clattering of horses' hoofs broke the silence and the Queen ran to the window. She smiled as two horses came to a halt far below her and only one rider dismounted.

Trembling, and beside himself with fear, the huntsman climbed the endless stairs to the Throne Room. As he bowed low before the Queen she snatched the jeweled casket with eager hands, turned the tiny key, and put back the lid.

"Ahhhh! The heart of a Princess!" she gloated, and turned abruptly on her spiked heels, dismissing the huntsman.

As she hurried down the seven corridors she was certain that now, at last, she was the fairest in the land. Jerking back the heavy draperies before her precious mirror, she cried:

"*NOW*, magic mirror on the wall, who is the fairest one of all?"

Green and yellow vapors hovered over the glass as the mirror replied:

"Beyond the seven mountains,
Beyond the seventh glen
Beyond the seven waterfalls
Live seven little men!"

"The Dwarfs!" she murmured, puzzled. "How does that answer my question?"

The voice of the mirror went on:

"With the dwarfs will spend the night
The fairest in the land--SNOW WHITE!"

She was unable to speak. She could only point to the heart lying in the jeweled box.

Slowly the mirror explained:

"The huntsman has tricked you!

'Tis the heart of a beast!"

The Queen grew livid with anger and raising her arm, hurled the box at the mirror, shattering it in a thousand pieces. A little laugh broke from each splinter of glass and grew and grew until her ears were filled with the mocking laughter.

In all her life she had never been in such a fury. She kicked and screamed with rage. Through her madness ran but one thought: *She would destroy the Princess herself!*

CHAPTER VII

The Queen's shadow hurried after her along the narrow damp walls of the tunnel, down many slippery steps, over a little bridge to a dark cave far below the palace. Turning a rusty key she pushed back the heavy door to her laboratory, where she concocted her Black Magic.

Her pet raven awoke to flap his wings, then settled back comfortably above the glowing embers of the fire.

Scanning a row of books the Queen selected one entitled MAGIC DISGUISES. She rustled back the pages, talking aloud to herself.

"First, a formula to transform my beauty into ugliness—my queenly raiment to a peddler's cloak!"

Strange ingredients made up the magic potion: Sands of Time, Black of Night, Crocodile Tears, Camel's Hump, Scream of Fright. She stirred them all together and when it was ready drank it off at one draught. The beautiful Queen disappeared and an old toothless hag covered in tattered rags stood in her place!

Her voice had changed to a rasping cackle when she spoke:

"And now for the Princess . . . what special sort of death for one so fair? . . . . the poisoned comb for her ebony hair?"

Turning the pages of her BOOK OF POISONS she shook her scraggly hair.

"The magic bodice to stifle her breath . . . ."

At last she stopped, a toothless grin stretched across her wrinkled face.

"Ah! Just the thing . . . . The poisoned apple . . . . the sleeping death . . . . perfect!" she gloated, laying the book open before her with a malicious chuckle.

CHAPTER VIII

Snow White and the dwarfs had forgotten all about the cruel Queen. The woods rang with their laughter, and the little birds and animals peeking in the windows beat time to their music. What music! Each one of the dwarfs had made himself an instrument after his own ideas, and the sound of those seven instruments playing together was different from anything you've ever heard.

Grumpy pumped away at a homemade organ with pipes like totem-poles intricately carved with birds and animals. Every time he pressed a key a wooden bird moved its wings up and down, or stretched open

its beak to let out weird sounds. There were fiddles with necks like swans and duck horns and fish horns with big staring eyes.

Happy led the orchestra and kept them all stepping and puffing and blowing. Snow White tapped her foot and clapped her hands in time to their yodel song.

"Oh! That was fun!" she gasped.

And what dancing! The bandy legs of the dwarfs skipped about with funny little steps in a funny little dance all their own. They even pulled Snow White to her feet and took turns whirling her around.

The seven little men were happier than they had been for three hundred years.

"Now you do something!" urged Happy bouncing up and down trying to pull Snow White from her chair where she had dropped exhausted from laughing and dancing.

"Saaay," yawned Sleepy. "Tell us a story."

"A true story," begged Happy.

"A lo-o-ve story," sighed Bashful.

"Mush!" snorted Grumpy.

Sitting in the light of the dim-glowing fire, encircled by the little men, Snow White smiled and said,

"Well, once there was a Princess."

"Was the Princess you?" interrupted Happy.

"And she fell in love," continued Snow White.

"Mush!" repeated Grumpy sitting alone in the shadow.

But Snow White paid no attention to him. She followed her thoughts in a far-away voice:

"Dreams . . . dreams are really magic, aren't they? I see myself in the loveliest gown, woven of moonlight and fairy wings."

The dwarfs listened . . . enchanted. They were carried off on a filmy mist to a starry sky where Snow White wandered through a meadow of shimmering star daisies, while in the distance her Prince, mounted on a white horse, galloped down the sky lanes towards her, waving his plumed hat.

Little stars clustered round her skirts as the Prince bowed low and kissed her hand. Impish little stars mimicked them, and lifting cupid bows, shot shafts of starlight after them as they galloped off together on the white horse.

In the low light of the dying fire the fairy mist faded away. Snow White sighed. And her sigh was echoed rapturously from the upturned faces of all seven of the fascinated dwarfs.

Suddenly a loud snore broke the charm. Sleepy was snoozing on the woodpile. Dopey gave the bottom log a kick and sent the woodpile and Sleepy tumbling to the floor. Sleepy woke up, blinked and said:

"Tell us a story."

Everybody laughed. Just then the clock flew open and an old frog came out to croak eleven.

"Heavens!" exclaimed Snow White. "It's way past bedtime! Run along upstairs, all of you!"

"Nay, my dear Princess!" said Doc, bowing gallantly and holding out the candle. "It is our pleasure that you should beep in our sleds—er, slip in our sheds, I mean sleep in our beds."

"But where will you sleep?" asked Snow White.

"Oh, we'll be very comfortable. We most always sleep downstairs, don't we, men? Yes indeed! It's so much warmer, isn't it, boys? You bet! Besides the bedroom roof leaks and it looks like rain tonight!"

"Well, if you insist . . . . Goodnight! Pleasant dreams!" called Snow White from the stairs.

Hardly had the bedroom door closed when the dwarfs made a dive for the only pillow in the room. What a scramble! clutching! pulling!

yanking! a snowstorm of feathers! When there was nothing left of the pillow for anyone, they all settled down to sleep. Dopey found one soft little feather, and put it carefully under his cheek before he closed his eyes.

Upstairs Snow White finished her prayers and was about to get into bed when she knelt down once more:

"Oh, yes . . . and please make Grumpy love me!"

CHAPTER IX

Far below the castle the ugly Queen worked in her secret room with only her pet raven for company.

Boil, cauldron, boil
Boil, cauldron, boil
Death within your depths I see
For one who dares to rival me
Brew the magic recipe
Boil, cauldron, boil!

The poison brew bubbled and boiled over the fire. Taking an apple from a basket she tied a string to the stem and lowered it into the poison. When she had done this three times the apple came out a beautiful rosy red and was the most tempting apple in all the world.

But suddenly the witchlike smile faded from the Queen's face. Hurrying to her BOOK OF POISONS she rustled back the pages. Perhaps there was an antidote for this poison—nothing must be overlooked!

"Ah! Just as I suspected . . . . . .*THE SLEEPING DEATH CAN ONLY BE BROKEN BY LOVE'S FIRST KISS!* . . . . Ha! the dwarfs will think her dead and bury her alive!"

Shrieking with laughter over her beautiful scheme, the disguised Queen took up her basket of apples and went out. She climbed into a little boat and pushed her way along the underground stream with a long pole. It was dawn as she skirted the last wall of the castle and came out on the river. Veiled by an early morning mist she shoved her boat into the bulrushes along the shore and disappeared in the woods.

By the time the sun was up the old hag had traveled far. And as she walked she muttered to herself in a strange tongue. Leaning heavily on her stick, she rested her basket of apples on the ground, and looking down from the seventh mountain, saw a thin spiral of smoke in the distance.

"That must be the dwarfs' chimney!" she muttered. "I'll be there by noon."

CHAPTER X

The next morning Snow White stood in the doorway of the cottage saying goodbye to the dwarfs as they went off to the mine.

"Now remember!" said Doc wagging his head, "the Queen's a sly one —fulla witchcraft—you be careful of strangers!"

"Oh! don't worry. I'll be all right," smiled Snow White, and reaching down she kissed him on top of the head. He bounced off along the path like a rubber ball and wanted to yell "WHEE" but had to remember his dignity.

She kissed each one as he said goodbye, warning her against the Queen.

"We wouldn't want anything to happen to our little Princess," said

Happy. "Heh-heh!—or our gooseberry pies!"

Snow White laughed and out of the corner of her eye she saw Grumpy hurriedly slicking himself up for his turn. Then, pretending not to notice her, he swaggered to the door.

"Now you listen to me!" he growled. "Keep the doors locked! If it's only a breeze, don't let it in. Not that I care a tinker's whoop about

you, but I don't want the house all mussed up!"

Bending down quickly Snow White gave him a big kiss. He jerked away and stormed off, but after he had gone a few steps his fierce scowl changed to a smile. He glanced back over his shoulder and Snow White threw him another kiss. Whirling around he went smack into a tree. Then, holding the bump on his nose, he slipped and fell in the brook. Dripping wet, he scrambled out and marched off in a terrible huff.

"Wimmin!" he sputtered, pulling a fish out of his pocket. "Just a bunch of bad luck. I hate 'em worse than pizen!"

The dwarfs didn't go to the mine. Grumpy found them sitting in the forest with their eyebrows pulled down, trying to think. They sat under a great oak and their picks lay idle on the ground. They were try-

ing to think of a present for Snow White—something to make her happy—something to show her how much they loved her.

Happy jumped up.

"I got it!" he said. "Let's make her a crown of precious jewels!"

"Naw!" they all said. "What do you want to do? Give her a headache?"

"I know just the thing," volunteered Doc. "A royal coach with six white horses!"

"Naw!" they booed. "She's not going anywhere!"

Again there was silence as they pondered.

"Why don't you make her a bed?" yawned Sleepy going right off to sleep again.

They all jumped up and shouted:

"A BED! PERFECT! THAT'S IT—A BED!"

In their enthusiasm they all tried to talk at once.

"I'll cut the posts."

"I'll carve the name."

"I'll carve angels all over the frame."

"I'll make the mattress good and stout."

"And I'll, I'll try it out!" put in Sleepy.

"If you want to spoil her, go ahead . . . make her a bed. Pah!" said Grumpy sourly.

And before long the forest rang with the shouts of the busy men chopping and sawing and hammering.

Grumpy staggered under the weight of a big board for the foot of the bed. Laying it in place, he quickly sketched in a design which served as a pattern which the woodpeckers carved with their beaks while the beavers gnawed the corners round and smooth.

Bashful was busy carving angels.

And in a near-by field of thistles, goldenrod, and dandelion blow, scores of birds gathered fluff and carried it in their beaks to Sneezy, who stuffed the mattress with it. Dopey came along with an armful of goldenrod which was too much for Sneezy. He ducked his head into the mattress with such an explosive sneeze that the mattress swelled up light and airy as a zeppelin.

Happy, using a tree for his tailoring shop, stitched away on the quilt. Spools of thread stood on little twigs like spindles, and a skein of bright wool was stretched between the antlers of a deer. Little birds flew back and forth unwinding the wool, while others snipped off lengths with their scissor-like beaks. Dopey brought up a supply of shirt tails which he had carefully swiped from the backs of the dwarf's shirts while they were busy working.

Doc lovingly set jewels—beautiful rubies and emeralds and sapphires—into the headboard to spell SNOW WHITE.

CHAPTER XI

All the while, humming a little tune, Snow White was very busy making beds and putting the house in order. Her friends, the birds and animals, came in to help. When everything was neat and tidy she mixed

the dough and rolled it out for gooseberry pies. Seven juicy pies! Each one with the name of a little dwarf written in the crust! Smiling with anticipation of his pleasure, Snow White was putting the finishing touches to Grumpy's pie when a shadow fell across the table. Looking up she saw an old hag at the window, her wrinkled face stretched in a toothless grin.

"All alone, my pet?" she cooed.

Forgetting the birds and animals outside, Snow White nodded.

"Why, why . . yes . . . I am."

"Smells good," sniffed the Queen, setting her basket of apples on the window-sill. "But apple-pies taste better! Delicious apples! Like to try one?" she said holding up the poison apple.

Snow White reached out her hand. Just then the animals and little

birds who had been watching from behind the trees, suddenly rushed upon the Queen and beat her back across the garden with wings and beaks and little claws. Running out of the house, Snow White shooed away the birds angrily.

"Stop it!—Go away!—Shame on you!"

She could not understand why her friends would behave so badly to a poor old peddler woman, so she helped her in the house and made her comfortable in a big chair.

A storm was brewing. Dark clouds raced across the sky. The birds beat wildly against the windowpane, and with frantic little cries tried to warn Snow White. But still she didn't understand. So they tore off through the woods to find the dwarfs. When the birds and animals burst upon them, they were just finishing the bed—a beautiful bed shining with jewels. The birds swooped down and grabbed the beards of the astonished little dwarfs and flew off with their hats.

"Git away . . . git away . . . shoo . . . .shoo . . " shouted Sneezy fighting them off.

"Stop . . . Let go of me . . . Let go! Pesky . . . Dod-blasted!" thundered Grumpy.

But Sleepy, appearing from the depths of the mattress, suggested that maybe the Queen had come.

"THE QUEEN" cried Grumpy. "She'll kill her . . . we gotta save her!"

In their excitement and confusion the dwarfs knocked each other down trying to jump on the backs of the animals. Grumpy mounted a deer and led the way while Dopey bobbed along at the end on a hare.

Meantime, sitting in the cottage rocking by the fire, the wily Queen had an idea. Feeling in her pocket she pulled out the poisoned apple.

"Because you've been so kind to a poor old body," she crooned, "I shall share a secret with you. This is a MAGIC WISHING APPLE! Take a bite as you make a wish and your dream will come true!"

"A wishing apple! Oh!" breathed Snow White, delighted. Closing her eyes tightly and thinking of her Prince, she whispered:

"I wish . . . . I wish . . ."

"Quick! Bite the apple before your wish gets cold!" cried the old hag.

Snow White bit into the apple and immediately the poison took effect. With one pitiful little cry she sank to the floor.

The horrible Queen hovered over her and cackled wildly:

"NOW I . . . . I AM THE FAIREST IN THE LAND!"

Heavy black clouds now hung low over the sky and a torrent of rain poured down. The Queen flung out of the house just as the dwarfs rushed into the clearing brandishing their picks.

"There she is . . . after her, men!" yelled Grumpy.

The Queen ran into the forest and the wind picked up the tattered rags of her disguise spreading them out behind her like the wings of a bat.

The chase was on—dwarfs, birds, animals driven along by the wind and the rain. Lightning flashed through the dark woods and the cries of the dwarfs were lost in the loud roll of thunder.

Suddenly, from the floor of the forest, a high cliff loomed before the fleeing Queen. She had no time to lose. Behind her the beat of the animals' hoofs thudded nearer and nearer. Hand over hand she scaled the huge rocks. When she looked down she saw the dwarfs scrambling up, up, up, close after her.

Crawling onto a barren shelf of rock, high above the trees, the Queen searched about for something to hurl down on her pursuers.

"I'm trapped—what'll I do—drat that pack of meddling little men!" she croaked.

Finding nothing at hand, she pushed with all her might against a huge boulder just above their heads, but a blinding flash of lightning startled her and she lost her balance and slipped, falling backwards over the precipice. Her wild screams gradually faded and trailed off in silence.

The dwarfs clambered to the top and crawled to the edge of the chasm. Far, far below lay the body of the hateful Queen. No magic could ever bring her to life again.

CHAPTER XII

When the dwarfs returned they found Snow White on the floor where she had fallen. And the cottage was strangely silent. The little men did everything they could think of to revive their beloved Princess, but finally with broken hearts they laid her gently on the table and placed two candles—one at her head and one at her feet. The flickering light cast huge shadows of the dwarfs upon the walls. Then they knelt in a circle around her, their upturned faces still and oh! so sad.

Outside the storm had passed over, but from the trees, down the windowpanes and off the roof, rain dripped like gentle tears. Here and there hushed groups of birds and animals huddled together wet and shivering.

Tears brimmed over the edge and ran slowly down Grumpy's leathery cheeks as a great sob shook his bent shoulders and echoed through the stillness.

Snow White looked so beautiful, she seemed to be only asleep, as she had been when they first found her. The little dwarfs could not bury her in the cold ground. So they built a glistening coffin of crystal and gold and placed her inside on a satin couch. They carried it to a grassy knoll in the depths of the forest, where tall old pine trees carpeted the ground with their fragrant needles. There they kept constant watch over her throughout the long winter months.

Meantime the lonely Prince wandered far and wide searching for his lost Princess. It was spring again when he heard of a beautiful maiden who slept in a glass coffin under the trees.

He traveled day and night through the forest and did not rest until he came out upon a little hill where a strange sight met his eyes. Birds showered flower petals from their beaks and little men laid wreaths of flowers around a glass coffin shining brightly in the sunlight.

There lay Snow White. She seemed to be only sleeping. Striding across the green, the Prince bent down and kissed her before the astonished dwarfs could speak. They just stood still and stared as Snow White stirred like a child waking from a deep sleep, and the evil spell was broken.

But when she saw the Prince and he took her in his arms smiling and happy, they all went wild with joy! The little dwarfs turned cartwheels and hugged each other, while the birds swelled their little throats to bursting with song.

They helped Snow White mount the Prince's white horse and he swung up lightly beside her—just as he had done in her dream. She blew kisses to all her friends and promised to return and visit them every spring. Then they rode away. From the top of the last hill they stopped once again to wave goodbye.

The little dwarfs were very happy as they watched her ride off beside her Prince, to his Castle of Dreams, because they knew it was her dream come true.